This Little Tiger book
belongs to:

_____

_____

_____

For Amy and Alicia
~ M S
For Kin and Tridge
~ L F

LITTLE TIGER PRESS LTD,
an imprint of the Little Tiger Group
1 Coda Studios, 189 Munster Road,
London SW6 6AW
www.littletiger.co.uk
First published in Great Britain 2019
This edition published 2019
Text copyright © Mark Sperring 2019
Illustrations copyright © Lucy Fleming 2019

Mark Sperring and Lucy Fleming have asserted
their rights to be identified as the author and illustrator of this
work under the Copyright, Designs and Patents Act, 1988

THE MOST WONDERFUL GIFT in the WORLD

Mark Sperring

Lucy Fleming

LITTLE TiGER
LONDON

It was Christmas morning and one last
present sat beneath the tree.
    "I bet it's mine!" giggled Esme.
    "No, mine!" whooped Bear.
But as they reached for the
red-wrapped gift, they noticed
something HUGELY surprising.
It wasn't for either one of them.
Not Esme . . . OR Bear!

The tag read *For Little Bunny Boo-Boo, Love Santa.*
"Well," said Esme, "in all the busy
JuMbLE - TuMbleNesS of Christmas, somebody's present
has been mixed up with ours."
BUT WHAT SHOULD THEY DO?

"Let's open it!" said Bear, giving it a BEARISH sniff.
Esme had a better idea. "Let's find Little Bunny Boo-Boo
and make sure she gets her gift!"

So they pulled on their
warm winter clothes and
set off into the snow.

They had not gone far when they
came across a sign.

FOR LITTLE BUNNY BOO-BOO'S
HOUSE, FOLLOW THE
TREACHEROUS
PATH

"The TREACHEROUS path!" gulped
Bear. "I don't like the sound of that!"
"How TREACHEROUS can it be?"
shrugged Esme, sure they'd both be fine.

But, OH DEAR! The path was VERY treacherous indeed!

With SLIPPY bits . . .

and SLIDEY bits . . . .

and FALL-DOWN-ON-YOUR-BOTTOM bits!

BUMP!

After much slip-sliding about,
they came across another sign.

FOR LITTLE BUNNY BOO-BOO'S
HOUSE, WALK THROUGH THE
HOWLING
GALE!

Bear looked worried, but Esme
gave him a comforting pat.
"How HOWLY can a gale
be?" she said.

But suddenly the wind picked up and
blasted them full in the face . . .

Arooooooo!

Arooooooool!

"Can't we just keep Bunny Boo-Boo's present and go back home?" begged Bear.

"Of course not!" called Esme over the GROWLING-HOWLING GALE.

Soon the wind died down,
and they came to the
last and final sign.

Little Bunny Boo-Boo's
house is just beyond the
DEEP, DEEP snow drifts.
WARNING:
THEY REALLY ARE
QUITE DEEP!

When the snow reached Esme's knees,
Bear scooped her high up onto his
shoulders and carried her, just like
that, for the rest of the way.

"Straight ahead for Bunny Boo-Boo's
house!" cheered Esme, as a twinkling
cabin came into view.

So Bear handed over the gift, and they all
huddled round to see what could be inside.
    "Maybe it's tiddlywinks!" smiled Esme.
    "Or peppermints!" beamed Bear.
    BUT imagine Esme and Bear's surprise when
Bunny Boo-Boo opened the gift and it was
ABSOLUTELY EMPTY with
NOTHING INSIDE AT ALL . . .

. . . except for a teeny-tiny handwritten note,
on the smallest scrap of paper.

Dear Little Bunny Boo-Boo,
here is exactly what
you asked for!

Love, Santa x

Little Bunny Boo-Boo stared at Esme and
Bear and her eyes grew wide with joy.
"I've just moved into my little cabin," she said,
"and I haven't had time to make a single friend.
So, this year, I asked Santa for a VERY special gift . . ."

"A friend (perhaps even two) who was honest and true, who would walk a TREACHEROUS PATH, battle the HOWLIEST of GALES, and brave the DEEPEST OF SNOW DRIFTS just to stand by my side."

"So you see!" smiled Bunny Boo-Boo, "Santa's present to me . . . IS YOU!"

"US?" said Esme and Bear, thinking that perhaps a skipping rope or spinning top might have been better!

But after they'd enjoyed a Christmas Day
full of laughter and lovely things to eat, they
all agreed that things like skipping ropes
and spinning tops were very nice but . . .
a TRUE friend (perhaps even two) was the
BEST and MOST WONDERFUL gift of all!

More snowy stories to share with little ones!

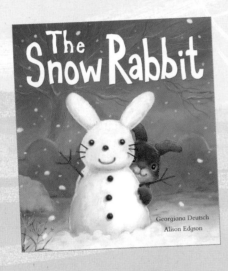

The **Snow Rabbit**

Georgiana Deutsch
Alison Edgson

I'll Love You For Ever

Owen Hart
Sean Julian

Barry Timms Ag Jatkowska

Santa to the Rescue!

With flaps to lift, LETTERS to open and a POP-UP surprise!

The Christmas EXTRAVAGANZA Hotel

TRACEY CORDEROY   TONY NEAL

One Christmas Journey

A Touch-and-feel book

M Christina Butler
Tina Macnaughton

Jane Chapman

The **Snowiest Christmas Ever!**

LiTTLE TiGER

For information regarding any of the above titles or for our catalogue, please contact us: Little Tiger Press Ltd, 1 Coda Studios, 189 Munster Road, London SW6 6AW · Tel: 020 7385 6333
E-mail: contact@littletiger.co.uk · www.littletiger.co.uk